HeartFelt Stories began with a dream fueled by the childlike enthusiasm that lives in the very heart of our souls. We've given life to our dream by creating a collection of stories and characters we hope will bring a smile to your face and have a permanent place in your heart. Our message is one of belief, not just the belief in a dream but a belief in yourself and your ability to follow that dream wherever it leads.

Thank You!

We appreciate and believe in you!
We hope our stories touch your heart.

Published by David Rastoka and Eric Klosky
Story Created and Written by Denise Bloom / Deana Froelich / David Rastoka
Illustrations by Kimo Tenorio

More Than a Spoonful

IdeaStream Consumer Products, LLC.

Printed in China.

For information, contact
HeartFelt Stories, LLC / PO Box 26094, Columbus, Ohio 43226
www.heartfeltstoriesllc.com

Library of Congress Control Number: 2006922442
Library of Congress Cataloging-in-Publication Data is available
ISBN 0-9778113-0-1– ISBN 13: 9-7809-778113-0-4

10 9 8 7 6 5 4 3 2

Follow Your Dream

Follow your dream;
face it with courage.
Don't get distracted;
don't get discouraged.
Store it in your heart,
deep down where dreams go.
Protect it and feed it;
allow it to grow.
Follow your dream,
and make it your mission.
When others say you can't,
just don't listen!
Believe in yourself
and all your know-how.
Life moves so fast;
the time is now.
Believe in yourself,
and to others be true.
And the dreams that you follow
will surely come true.

-Denise Bloom

More Than a Spoonful

HeartFelt Stories

touching hearts & shaping minds

On the table lies little Spooner,
waiting to be used not later but sooner.

He watched as Spike,
his forkly neighbor,
snatched up peas
with little labor.

He wondered why Spike seemed so able
to pick up peas across the table.

When he tried he wasn't so lucky;
his peas got smooshed into green pea yucky!

Then one day Spooner decided to ask
about this not-so-simple task.
Spike replied, "I use my tines to pick up food.
How about you? What do you use, dude?"

Spooner said, "I have no tines. Am I disabled because I can't poke food up from the table?"

Spike looked at Spooner and thought a minute
about what really made them different.
He thought and thought and thought some more
about all the things spoons are used for.

Spike turned to Spooner and gave him a smile,
and said to him in a very sharp style,
"YES, when it comes to tines, I've got you beat,
but you can do things in which I can't even compete!

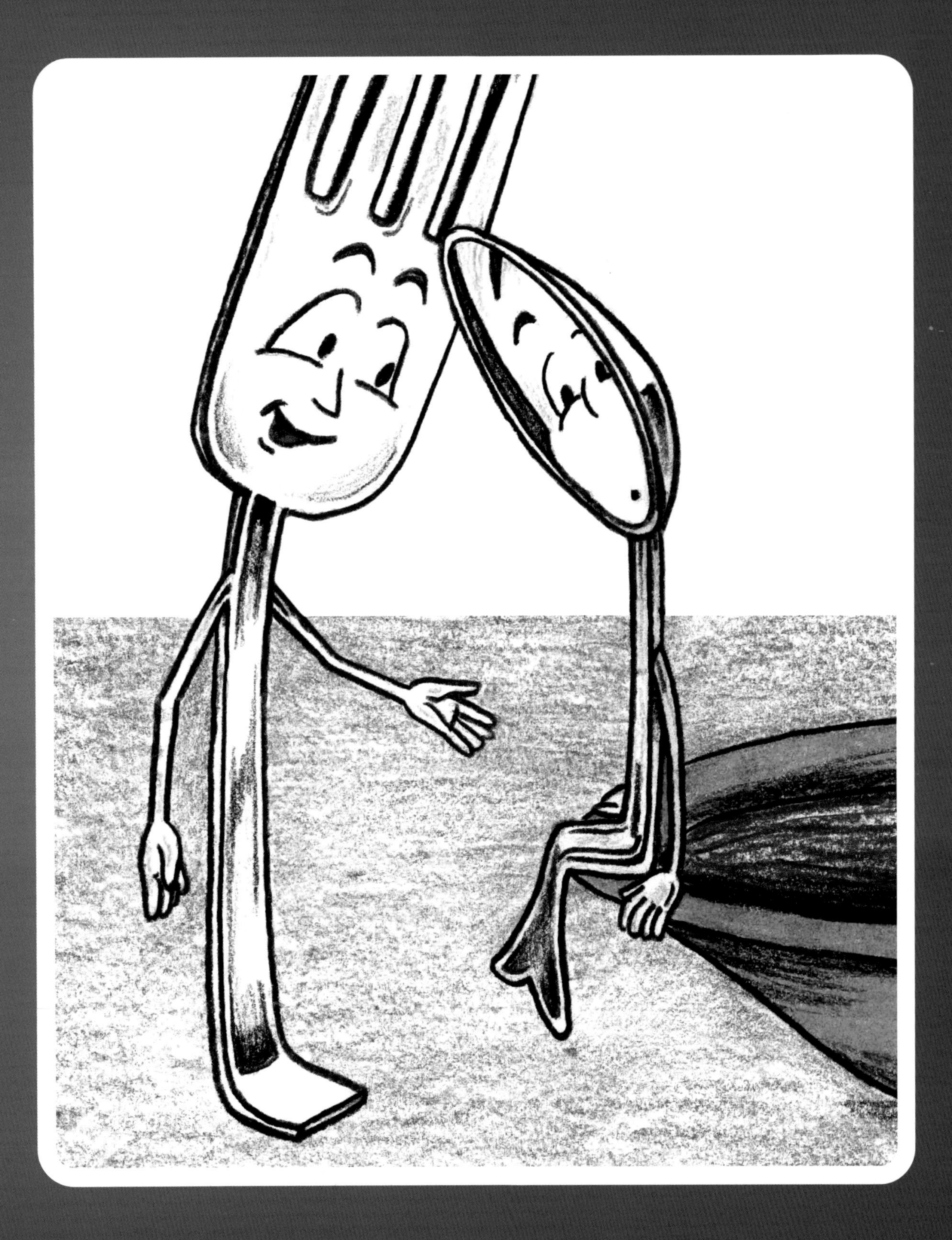

You can scoop up some soup,
some sugar, some salt,
and serve pudding and cereal
with hardly a fault.

You can grab
ice cream
without any
drips and
help me twirl
spaghetti so you
don't have to sip!

I have watched you and I've been astounded.
Face it my friend, you're quite well rounded!
You have many a gift that you do not see
because you're too busy looking at me.
Look at yourself and what you can do;
be proud and be happy for you're special too!"

Spooner exhaled a sigh of relief
and finally realized that being different is sweet!
He then lay next to Spike and stared at the sky
and thought about all the times he used to ask, "WHY?"

“We all have gifts, don’t we Spike?
And it’s so cool that we’re not all alike!”
Then someone joined them on the table nearby,
someone quite different, but now Spooner knew why.

Jin-Jin the chopsticks just
smiled and said, “Hi!”

Kimo Tenorio...
Who am I?
I am just a regular guy
who loves his
wife Alison and two kids,
Jesse and Mariah.
I love to play with my
kids and their friends too!
I believe in honor
of family, friends
and country.
Being a good American
is everything!
Illustrating the words
of these talented writers
at HeartFelt Stories
has let me release
the kid in me!

Deana Froelich
has always had a
passion for the
welfare of children
and animals.
Besides a career as a
writer and author,
she is an adjunct
faculty member in the
developmental
education department
of a local college.
She has worked in the
social services sector
on behalf of children
and adopted
unwanted dogs from
local animal shelters.
She's spent most of
her adult life in
Los Angeles, California,
and holds a Master
of Education from
Pepperdine University.
Deana currently resides
in Columbus, Ohio,
with her two adopted
dogs, Bono and Evie.

Denise Bloom
is a poet...
and is happy now
that she finally
gets to show it!
Her hometown of
Cleveland has a
piece of her heart...
but, her home's now
in Columbus,
where she got
a fresh start...
with her husband, Jeff
and daughter,
Amanda too
and their two kitty cats
to round off their crew.
She likes all things
creative...
especially to cook,
and hopes to win
the Pillsbury bake-off
if enough buy this book!
She's been in retail
management for
what seems like forever...
and this book is
a testament to
"Never say never!"

David Rastoka
was born in
Cleveland, Ohio,
and has worked with
people with disabilities
for the past 24 years.
He has a passion for
children and truly
enjoys their innocence
and energy.
Dave believes
that there are two kinds
of people in the world,
spectators and
participants.
Being a participant in
life means taking
risks and following
your dreams.
Dave is also a
motivational speaker;
his session entitled
"You're Walking, Talking
and Breathing But Are
You Really Alive?"
discusses his 10 Rules
for a Happy Life!
He currently resides in
Powell, Ohio.

A HeartFelt thank you to Tony DeCarlo and Eric Klosky
for their help in making our dream a reality. Without their knowledge, expertise and,
most importantly, their friendship, none of this would have been possible.
We love you, Cumbi!
